Boy, Bird, and Dog

by David McPhail

I Like to Read™

Holiday House / New York

Library of Congress Cataloging-in-Publication Data
McPhail, David, 1940-
Boy, Bird, and Dog / by David McPhail. — 1st ed.
p. cm.
Summary: In this story for beginning readers, Boy, Bird, and Dog have lots of fun in their tree house.
ISBN 978-0-8234-2346-0 (hardcover)
[1. Tree houses—Fiction. 2. Dogs—Fiction. 3. Birds—Fiction.] I. Title.
PZ7.M478818Bo 2011
[E]—dc22
2010029435

Boy saw Bird.

Bird was up.

Boy went up.

"Hello, Boy," said Bird.

"Hello, Bird," said Boy.

They saw and saw.

Dog saw Bird and Boy.

"I want to go up," said Dog.

"But I can't."

Boy went down.

He got a rope.

He got a pot.

Dog went in the pot.

Boy went up.

He pulled the rope.

Dog was up.

"Hello, Dog," said Bird.

"Hello, Bird," said Dog.

Boy, Bird, and Dog liked to be up.

They saw and saw.

They saw Mom.

She went to the tree.

Mom had cookies.
She held them up,
but Boy did not go down.

He sent the pot.

Mom put the cookies in the pot.

Boy pulled up the pot.

Boy, Bird, and Dog had cookies.

Yum. They were good.

Boy, Bird, and Dog were happy!